William Crookes

On radiant matter: a lecture delivered to the British Association for the Advancement of Science, at Sheffield, Friday, August 22, 1879

Antigonos

William Crookes

On radiant matter: a lecture delivered to the British Association for the Advancement of Science, at Sheffield, Friday, August 22, 1879

Reprint of the original, first published in 1879.

1st Edition 2024 | ISBN: 978-3-38801-033-5

Antigonos Verlag is an imprint of Outlook Verlagsgesellschaft mbH.

Verlag (Publisher): Outlook Verlag GmbH, Zeilweg 44, 60439 Frankfurt, Deutschland, info@outlook-verlag.de
Vertretungsberechtigt (Authorized to represent): E. Roepke, Zeilweg 44, 60439 Frankfurt, Deutschland
Druck (Print): Libri Plureos GmbH, Friedensallee 273, 22763 Hamburg, Deutschland

ON

RADIANT MATTER.

A LECTURE DELIVERED

TO THE

BRITISH ASSOCIATION FOR THE ADVANCEMENT
OF SCIENCE,

AT SHEFFIELD,

FRIDAY, AUGUST 22, 1879.

BY

WILLIAM CROOKES, F.R.S.

RADIANT MATTER.

TO throw light on the title of this lecture I must go back more than sixty years—to 1816. Faraday, then a mere student and ardent experimentalist, was 24 years old, and at this early period of his career he delivered a series of lectures on the General Properties of Matter, and one of them bore the remarkable title, *On Radiant Matter*. The great philosopher's notes of this lecture are to be found in Dr. Bence Jones's *Life and Letters of Faraday*, and I will here quote a passage in which he first employs the expression *Radiant Matter*:—

"If we conceive a change as far beyond vaporisation as that is above fluidity, and then take into account also the proportional increased extent of alteration as the changes rise, we shall perhaps, if we can form any conception at all, not fall far short of Radiant Matter; and as in the last conversion many qualities were lost, so here also many more would disappear."

Faraday was evidently engrossed with this far-reaching speculation, for three years later—in 1819—we find him bringing fresh evidence and argument to strengthen his startling hypothesis. His notes are now more extended, and they show that in the intervening three years he had thought much and deeply on this higher form of matter. He first points out that matter may be classed into four states—solid, liquid, gaseous, and radiant—these modifications depending upon differences in their several essential properties. He admits that the existence of Radiant Matter is as yet unproved, and then proceeds, in a series of ingenious analogical arguments, to show the probability of its existence.*

* "I may now notice a curious progression in physical properties accompanying changes of form, and which is perhaps sufficient to induce, in the inventive and sanguine philosopher, a considerable degree of

If, in the beginning of this century, we had asked, What is a Gas? the answer then would have been that it is matter, expanded and rarefied to such an extent as to be impalpable, save when set in violent motion ; invisible, incapable of assuming or of being reduced into any definite form like solids, or of forming drops like liquids; always ready to expand where no resistance is offered, and to contract on being subjected to pressure. Sixty years ago such were the chief attributes assigned to gases. Modern research, however, has greatly enlarged and modified our views on the constitution of these elastic fluids. Gases are now considered to be composed of an almost infinite number of small particles or molecules, which are constantly moving in every direction with velocities of all conceivable magnitudes. As these molecules are exceedingly numerous, it follows that no molecule can move far in any direction without coming in contact with some other molecule. But if we exhaust the air or gas contained in a closed vessel, the number of molecules becomes diminished, and the distance through which any one of them can move without coming in contact with another is increased, the length of the mean free path being inversely proportional to the number of molecules present. The further this process is carried the longer becomes the average distance a molecule can travel before entering

---

belief in the association of the radiant form with the others in the set of changes I have mentioned.

" As we ascend from the solid to the fluid and gaseous states, physical properties diminish in number and variety, each state losing some of those which belonged to the preceding state. When solids are converted into fluids, all the varieties of hardness and softness are necessarily lost. Crystalline and other shapes are destroyed. Opacity and colour frequently give way to a colourless transparency, and a general mobility of particles is conferred.

" Passing onward to the gaseous state, still more of the evident characters of bodies are annihilated. The immense differences in their weight almost disappear; the remains of difference in colour that were left, are lost. Transparency becomes universal, and they are all elastic. They now form but one set of substances, and the varieties of density, hardness, opacity, colour, elasticity and form, which render the number of solids and fluids almost infinite, are now supplied by a few slight variations in weight, and some unimportant shades of colour.

" To those, therefore, who admit the radiant form of matter, no difficulty exists in the simplicity of the properties it possesses, but rather an argument in their favour. These persons show you a gradual resignation of properties in the matter we can appreciate as the matter ascends in the scale of forms, and they would be surprised if that effect were to cease at the gaseous state. They point out the greater exertions which Nature makes at each step of the change, and think that, consistently, it ought to be greatest in the passage from the gaseous to the radiant form."—*Life and Letters of Faraday,* vol. i., p. 308.

into collision; or, in other words, the longer its mean free
path, the more the physical properties of the gas or air are
modified. Thus, at a certain point, the phenomena of the
radiometer become possible, and on pushing the rarefaction
still further, *i.e.*, decreasing the number of molecules in a
given space and lengthening their mean free path, the expe-
rimental results are obtainable to which I am now about to
call your attention. So distinct are these phenomena from
anything which occurs in air or gas at the ordinary tension,
that we are led to assume that we are here brought face to
face with Matter in a Fourth state or condition, a condition
as far removed from the state of gas as a gas is from a liquid.

Mean Free Path.   Radiant Matter.

I have long believed that a well-known appearance observed in vacuum tubes is closely related to the phenomena
of the mean free path of the molecules. When the negative
pole is examined while the discharge from an induction-coil
is passing through an exhausted tube, a dark space is seen
to surround it. This dark space is found to increase
and diminish as the vacuum is varied, in the same way that
the mean free path of the molecules lengthens and contracts.
As the one is perceived by the mind's eye to get greater, so
the other is seen by the bodily eye to increase in size; and if
the vacuum is insufficient to permit much play of the molecules before they enter into collision, the passage of electricity shows that the " dark space " has shrunk to small
dimensions. We naturally infer that the dark space is
the mean free path of the molecules of the residual gas,
an inference confirmed by experiment.

I will endeavour to render this " dark space " visible to
all present. Here is a tube, (Fig. 1), having a pole in the

Fig. 1.

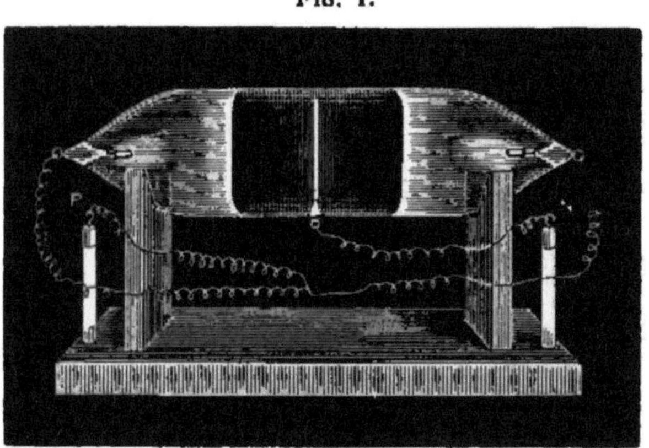

centre in the form of a metal disk, and other poles at each end. The centre pole is made negative, and the two end poles connected together are made the positive terminal. The dark space will be in the centre. When the exhaustion is not very great the dark space extends only a little on each side of the negative pole in the centre. When the exhaustion is good, as in the tube before you, and I turn on the coil, the dark space is seen to extend for about an inch on each side of the pole.

Here, then, we see the induction spark actually illuminating the lines of molecular pressure caused by the excitement of the negative pole. The thickness of this dark space is the measure of the mean free path between successive collisions of the molecules of the residual gas. The extra velocity with which the negatively electrified molecules rebound from the excited pole keeps back the more slowly moving molecules which are advancing towards that pole. A conflict occurs at the boundary of the dark space, where the luminous margin bears witness to the energy of the discharge.

Therefore the residual gas—or, as I prefer to call it, the gaseous residue—within the dark space is in an entirely different state to that of the residual gas in vessels at a lower degree of exhaustion. To quote the words of our last year's President, in his Address at Dublin :—

"In the exhausted column we have a vehicle for electricity not constant like an ordinary conductor, but itself modified by the passage of the discharge, and perhaps subject to laws differing materially from those which it obeys at atmospheric pressure."

In the vessels with the lower degree of exhaustion, the length of the mean free path of the molecules is exceedingly small as compared with the dimensions of the bulb, and the properties belonging to the ordinary gaseous state of matter, depending upon constant collisions, can be observed. But in the phenomena now about to be examined, so high is the exhaustion carried that the dark space around the negative pole has widened out till it entirely fills the tube. By great rarefaction the mean free path has become so long that the hits in a given time in comparison to the misses may be disregarded, and the average molecule is now allowed to obey its own motions or laws without interference. The mean free path, in fact, is comparable to the dimensions of the vessel, and we have no longer to deal with a *continuous* portion of matter, as would be the case were the tubes less highly exhausted, but we must here contemplate the molecules *individually*. In these highly exhausted vessels the molecules of the gaseous residue are able to dart across the tube with comparatively few collisions, and radiating from the pole with enormous velocity, they assume properties so novel and so characteristic as to entirely justify the application of the term borrowed from Faraday, that of *Radiant Matter*.

Radiant Matter exerts powerful phosphorogenic action where it strikes.

I have mentioned that the Radiant Matter within the dark space excites luminosity where its velocity is arrested by residual gas outside the dark space. But if no residual gas is left, the molecules will have their velocity arrested by the sides of the glass; and here we come to the first and one of the most noteworthy properties of Radiant Matter discharged from the negative pole—its power of exciting phosphorescence when it strikes against solid matter. The number of bodies which respond luminously to this molecular bombardment is very great, and the resulting colours are of every variety. Glass, for instance, is highly phosphorescent when exposed to a stream of Radiant Matter. Here (Fig. 2) are three bulbs

Fig. 2.

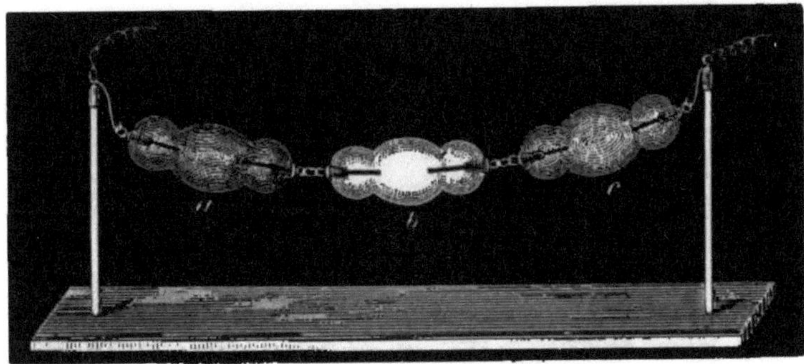

composed of different glass: one is uranium glass (*a*), which phosphoresces of a dark green colour; another is English glass (*b*), which phosphoresces of a blue colour; and the third (*c*) is soft German glass,—of which most of the apparatus before you is made,—which phosphoresces of a bright apple-green.

My earlier experiments were almost entirely carried on by the aid of the phosphorescence which glass takes up when it is under the influence of the radiant discharge; but many other substances possess this phosphorescent power in a still higher degree than glass. For instance, here is some of the luminous sulphide of calcium prepared according to M. Ed. Becquerel's description. When the sulphide is exposed to light—even candlelight—it phosphoresces for hours with a bluish white colour. It is, however, much more strongly phosphorescent to the molecular discharge in a good vacuum, as you will see when I pass the discharge through this tube.

Other substances besides English, German, and uranium glass, and Becquerel's luminous sulphides, are also phosphorescent. The rare mineral Phenakite (aluminate of glucinum) phosphoresces blue; the mineral Spodumene (a silicate of aluminium and lithium) phosphoresces a rich golden yellow; the emerald gives out a crimson light. But without exception, the diamond is the most sensitive substance I have yet met for ready and brilliant phosphorescence. Here is a very curious fluorescent diamond, green by daylight, colourless by candlelight. It is mounted in the centre of an exhausted bulb (Fig. 3),

Fig. 3.

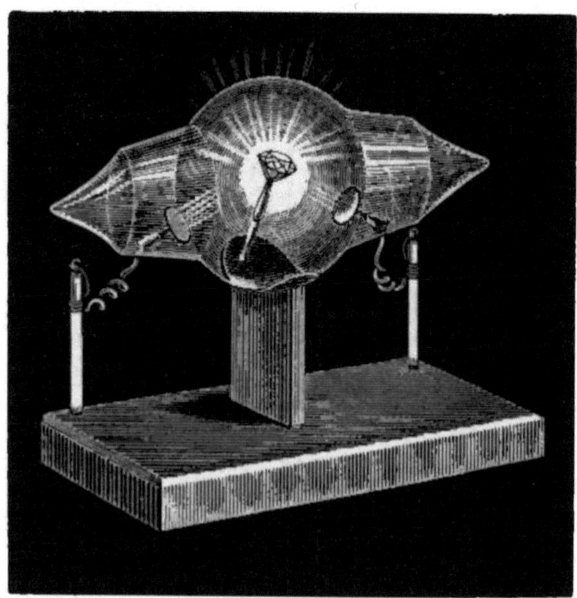

and the molecular discharge will be directed on it from below upwards. On darkening the room you see the diamond shines with as much light as a candle, phosphorescing of a bright green.

Next to the diamond the ruby is one of the most remarkable stones for phosphorescing. In this tube (Fig. 4) is a fine collection of ruby pebbles. As soon as the induction spark is

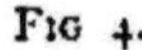
Fig 4.

turned on you will see these rubies shining with a brilliant rich red tone, as if they were glowing hot. It scarcely matters what colour the ruby is, to begin with. In this tube of natural rubies there are stones of all colours—the deep red and also the pale pink ruby. There are some so pale as to be almost colourless, and some of the highly-prized tint of pigeon's blood; but under the impact of Radiant Matter they all phosphoresce with about the same colour.

Now the ruby is nothing but crystallised alumina with a little colouring-matter. In a paper by Ed. Becquerel,* published twenty years ago, he describes the appearance of alumina as glowing with a rich red colour in the phosphoroscope. Here is some precipitated alumina prepared in the most careful manner. It has been heated to whiteness, and you see it also glows under the molecular discharge with the same rich red colour.

The spectrum of the red light emitted by these varieties of alumina is the same as described by Becquerel twenty years ago. There is one intense red line, a little below the fixed line B in the spectrum, having a wavelength of about 6895. There is a continuous spectrum beginning at about B, and a few fainter lines beyond it, but they are so faint in comparison with this red line that they

* Annales de Chimie et de Physique, 3rd series, vol. lvii., p. 50, 1859.

may be neglected. This line is easily seen by examining with a small pocket spectroscope the light reflected from a good ruby.

There is one particular degree of exhaustion more favourable than any other for the development of the properties of Radiant Matter which are now under examination. Roughly speaking it may be put at the millionth of an atmosphere.* At this degree of exhaustion the phosphorescence is very strong, and after that it begins to diminish until the spark refuses to pass.†

*

1·0 millionth of an atmosphere	=	0·00076 millim.
1315·789 millionths of an atmosphere	=	1·0 millim.
1,000,000· „ „ „	=	760·0 millims.
„ „ „ „	=	1 atmosphere.

† Nearly 100 years ago Mr. Wm. Morgan communicated to the Royal Society a Paper entitled " Electrical Experiments made to ascertain the Non-conducting Power of a Perfect Vacuum, &c." The following extracts from this Paper, which was published in the Phil. Trans. for 1785 (vol. lxxv., p. 272), will be read with interest :—

" A mercurial gage about 15 inches long, carefully and accurately boiled till every particle of air was expelled from the inside, was coated with tin-foil 5 inches down from its sealed end, and being inverted into mercury through a perforation in the brass cap which covered the mouth of the cistern ; the whole was cemented together, and the air was exhausted from the inside of the cistern through a valve in the brass cap, which producing a perfect vacuum in the gage formed an instrument peculiarly well adapted for experiments of this kind. Things being thus adjusted (a small wire having been previously fixed on the inside of the cistern to form a communication between the brass cap and the mercury, into which the gage was inverted) the coated end was applied to the conductor of an electrical machine, and notwithstanding every effort, neither the smallest ray of light, nor the slightest charge, could ever be procured in this exhausted gage."

" If the mercury in the gage be imperfectly boiled, the experiment will not succeed ; but the colour of the electric light, which in air rarefied by an exhauster is always violet or purple, appears in this case of a beautiful green, and, what is very curious, the degree of the air's rarefaction may be nearly determined by this means ; for I have known instances, during the course of these experiments, where a small particle of air having found its way into the tube, the electric light became visible, and as usual of a green colour; but the charge being often repeated, the gage has at length cracked at its sealed end, and in consequence the external air, by being admitted into the inside, has gradually produced a change in the electric light from green to blue, from blue to indigo, and so on to violet and purple, till the medium has at length become so dense as no longer to be a conductor of electricity. I think there can be little doubt, from the above experiments, of the non-conducting power of a perfect vacuum."

" This seems to prove that there is a limit even in the rarefaction of air, which sets bounds to its conducting power ; or, in other words, that the particles of air may be so far separated from each other as no longer to be able to transmit the electric fluid ; that if they are brought within a certain distance of each other, their conducting power begins, and continually increases till their approach also arrives at its limit."

I have here a tube (Fig. 5) which will serve to illustrate the dependence of the phosphorescence of the glass

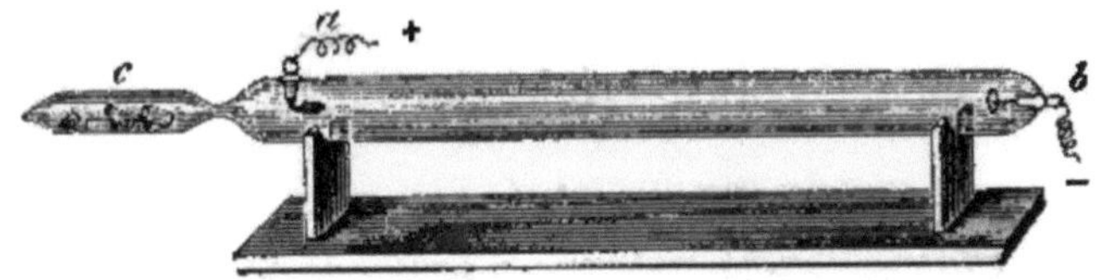

FIG. 5.

on the degree of exhaustion. The two poles are at *a* and *b*, and at the end (*c*) is a small supplementary tube connected with the other by a narrow aperture, and containing solid caustic potash. The tube has been exhausted to a very high point, and the potash heated so as to drive off moisture and injure the vacuum. Exhaustion has then been re-commenced, and the alternate heating and exhaustion repeated until the tube has been brought to the state in which it now appears before you. When the induction spark is first turned on nothing is visible—the vacuum is so high that the tube is non-conducting. I now warm the potash slightly and liberate a trace of aqueous vapour. Instantly conduction commences, and the green phosphorescence flashes out along the length of the tube. I continue the heat, so as to drive off more gas from the potash. The green gets fainter, and now a wave of cloudy luminosity sweeps over the tube, and stratifications appear, which rapidly get narrower, until the spark passes along the tube in the form of a narrow purple line. I take the lamp away, and allow the potash to cool; as it cools, the aqueous vapour, which the heat had driven off, is re-absorbed. The purple line broadens out, and breaks up into fine stratifications; these get wider, and travel towards the potash tube. Now a wave of green light appears on the glass at the other end, sweeping on and driving the last pale stratification into the potash ; and now the tube glows over its whole length with the green phosphorescence. I might keep it before you, and show the green growing fainter and the vacuum becoming non-conducting; but I should detain you too long, as time is required for the absorption of the last traces of vapour by the potash, and I must pass on to the next subject.

Radiant Matter proceeds in straight lines.

The Radiant Matter whose impact on the glass causes an evolution of light, absolutely refuses to turn a corner. Here is a V-shaped tube (Fig. 6), a pole being at each extremity. The pole at the right side (*a*) being negative, you

FIG. 6.

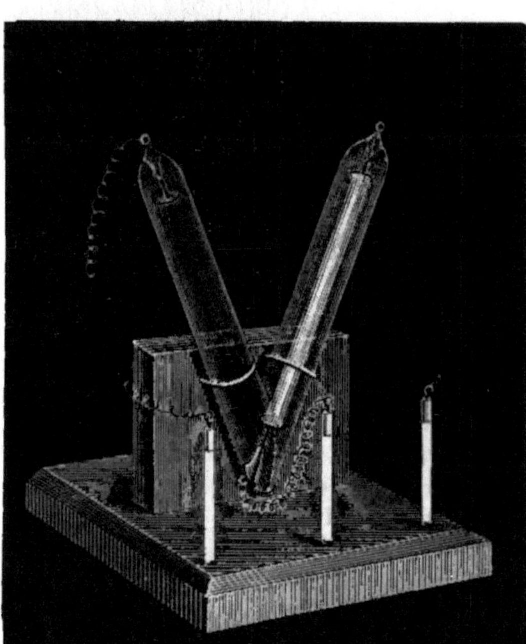

see that the whole of the right arm is flooded with green light, but at the bottom it stops sharply and will not turn the corner to get into the left side. When I reverse the current and make the left pole negative, the green changes to the left side, always following the negative pole and leaving the positive side with scarcely any luminosity.

In the ordinary phenomena exhibited by vacuum tubes—phenomena with which we are all familiar—it is customary, in order to bring out the striking contrasts of colour, to bend the tubes into very elaborate designs. The luminosity caused by the phosphorescence of the residual gas follows all the convolutions into which skilful glass-blowers can manage to twist the glass. The negative pole being at one end and the positive pole at the other, the luminous phenomena seem to depend more on the positive than on the negative at the ordinary exhaustion hitherto used to get the best phenomena of vacuum tubes. But at a very high exhaustion the phenomena noticed in ordinary vacuum tubes when the induction spark passes through them—an appearance of cloudy luminosity and of stratifications— disappear entirely. No cloud or fog whatever is seen in the body of the tube, and with such a vacuum as I am working with in these experiments, the only light observed is that from the phosphorescent surface of the glass. I have here two bulbs (Fig. 7), alike in shape and position

Fig. 7.

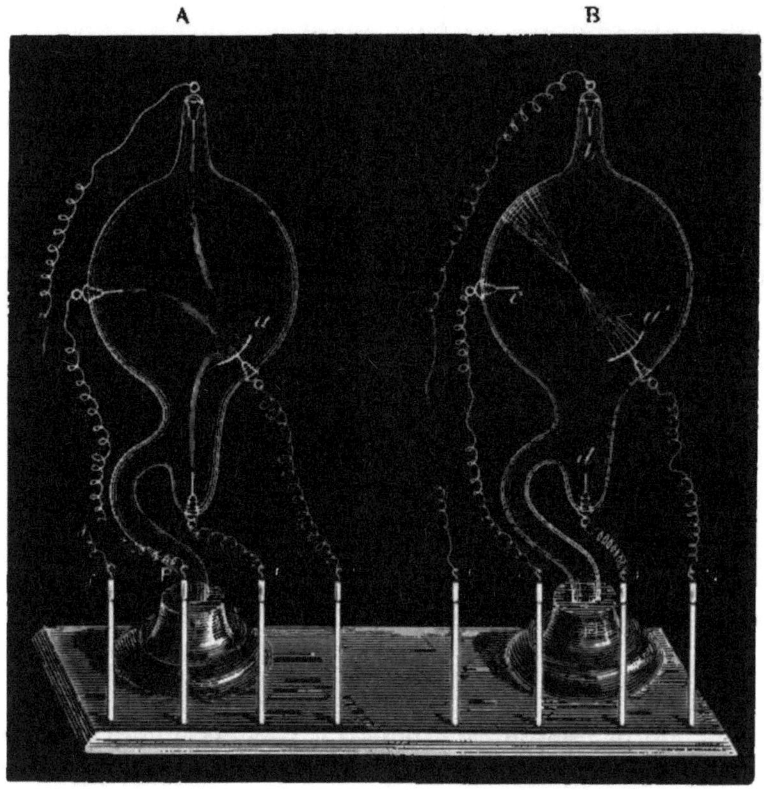

of poles, the only difference being that one is at an exhaustion equal to a few millimetres of mercury—such a moderate exhaustion as will give the ordinary luminous phenomena—whilst the other is exhausted to about the millionth of an atmosphere. I will first connect the moderately exhausted bulb (A) with the induction-coil, and retaining the pole at one side (*a*) always negative, I will put the positive wire successively to the other poles with which the bulb is furnished. You see that as I change the position of the positive pole, the line of violet light joining the two poles changes, the electric current always choosing the shortest path between the two poles, and moving about the bulb as I alter the position of the wires.

This, then, is the kind of phenomenon we get in ordinary exhaustions. I will now try the same experiment with a bulb (B) that is very highly exhausted, and as before, will make the side pole (*a'*) the negative, the top pole (*b*) being positive. Notice how widely different is the appearance from that shown by the last bulb. The negative pole is in the form of a shallow cup. The molecular rays from the cup cross in the centre of the bulb, and thence diverging fall on the opposite side and produce a circular patch of green phosphorescent light. As I turn the bulb round you will all be able to see the green patch on the glass. Now observe, I remove the positive wire from the top, and connect it with the side pole (*c*). The green patch from the divergent negative focus is there still. I now make the lowest pole (*d*) positive, and the green patch remains where it was at first, unchanged in position or intensity.

We have here another property of Radiant Matter. In the low vacuum the position of the positive pole is of every importance, whilst in a high vacuum the position of the positive pole scarcely matters at all; the phenomena seem to depend entirely on the negative pole. If the negative pole points in the direction of the positive, all very well, but if the negative pole is entirely in the opposite direction it is of little consequence : the Radiant Matter darts all the same in a straight line from the negative.

If, instead of a flat disk, a hemi-cylinder is used for the negative pole, the Matter still radiates normal to its surface. The tube before you (Fig. 8) illustrates this property. It contains, as a negative pole, a hemi-cylinder (*a*) of polished aluminium. This is connected with a fine copper wire, *b*, ending at the platinum terminal, *c*. At the upper end of the tube is another terminal, *d*. The induction-coil is connected so that the hemi-cylinder is negative and the upper pole positive, and when exhausted to a sufficient extent the projection of the molecular rays to a focus is very beautifully shown. The rays of Matter being driven from the hemi-cylinder in a direction normal to its surface, come to a focus and then diverge, tracing their path in brilliant green phosphorescence on the surface of the glass.

FIG. 8.

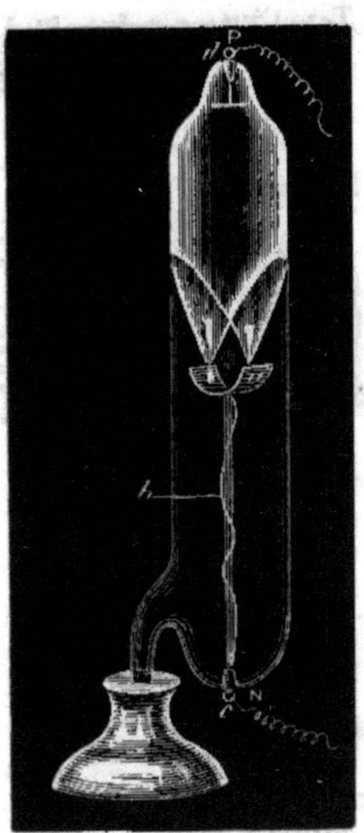

Instead of receiving the molecular rays on the glass, I will show you another tube in which the focus falls on a phosphorescent screen. See how brilliantly the lines of discharge shine out, and how intensely the focal point is illuminated, lighting up the table.

Radiant Matter when intercepted by solid matter casts a shadow.

Radiant Matter comes from the pole in straight lines, and does not merely permeate all parts of the tube and fill it with light, as would be the case were the exhaustion less good. Where there is nothing in the way the rays strike the screen and produce phosphorescence, and where solid matter intervenes they are obstructed by it, and a shadow is thrown on the screen. In this pear-shaped bulb (Fig. 9) the negative pole (*a*) is at the pointed end. In the middle is a

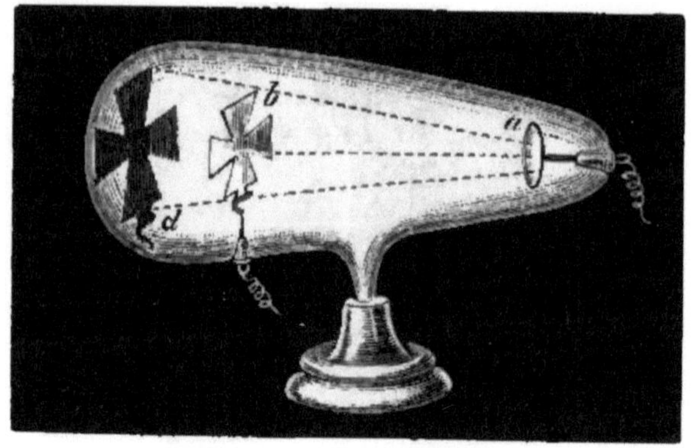

FIG. 9

cross (*b*) cut out of sheet aluminium, so that the rays from the negative pole projected along the tube will be partly intercepted by the aluminium cross, and will project an image of it on the hemispherical end of the tube which is phosphorescent. I turn on the coil, and you will all see the black shadow of the cross on the luminous end of the bulb (*c, d*). Now, the Radiant Matter from the negative pole has been passing by the side of the aluminium cross to produce the shadow; the glass has been hammered and bombarded till it is appreciably warm, and at the same time another effect has been produced on the glass—its sensibility has been deadened. The glass has got tired, if I may use the expression, by the enforced phosphorescence. A change has been produced by this molecular bombardment which will prevent the glass from responding easily to additional excitement; but the part that the shadow has fallen on is not tired—it has not been phosphorescing at all and is perfectly fresh; therefore if I throw down this cross,—I can easily do so by giving the apparatus a slight jerk, for it has been most ingeniously constructed with a hinge by Mr. Gimingham,—and so allow the rays from the negative pole to fall uninterruptedly on to the end of the bulb, you will suddenly see the black cross (*c, d*, Fig. 10) change to a luminous one (*e, f*), because the background is now only capable of faintly phosphorescing, whilst the part which had the black shadow on it retains its full phosphorescent power. The stencilled image of the luminous cross unfortunately soon dies out. After a period of rest the glass partly recovers its power of phosphorescing, but it is never so good as it was at first.

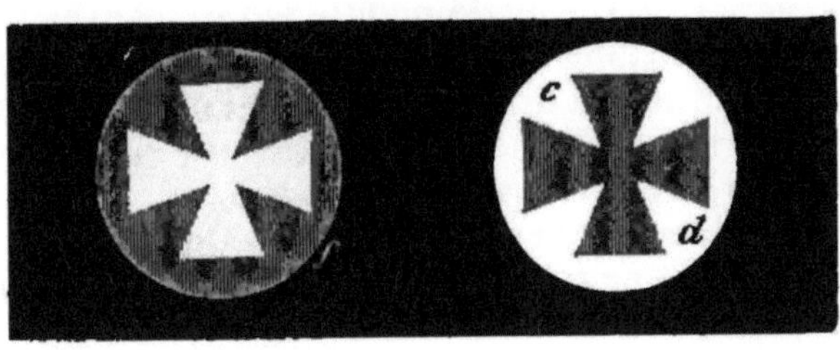

Fig. 10.

Here, therefore, is another important property of Radiant Matter. It is projected with great velocity from the negative pole, and not only strikes the glass in such a way as to cause it to vibrate and become temporarily luminous while the discharge is going on, but the molecules hammer away with sufficient energy to produce a permanent impression upon the glass.

Radiant Matter exerts strong mechanical action where it strikes.

We have seen, from the sharpness of the molecular shadows, that Radiant Matter is arrested by solid matter placed in its path. If this solid body is easily moved the impact of the molecules will reveal itself in strong mechanical action. Mr. Gimingham has constructed for me an ingenious piece of apparatus which when placed in the electric lantern will render this mechanical action visible to all present. It consists of a highly-exhausted glass tube (Fig. 11), having

Fig. 11.

a little glass railway running along it from one end to the other. The axle of a small wheel revolves on the rails, the

spokes of the wheel carrying wide mica paddles. At each
end of the tube, and rather above the centre, is an aluminium
pole, so that whichever pole is made negative the stream of
Radiant Matter darts from it along the tube, and striking
the upper vanes of the little paddle-wheel causes it to turn
round and travel along the railway. By reversing the poles
I can arrest the wheel and send it the reverse way, and if I
gently incline the tube the force of impact is observed to be
sufficient even to drive the wheel up-hill.

This experiment therefore shows that the molecular
stream from the negative pole is able to move any light
object in front of it.

The molecules being driven violently from the pole there
should be a recoil of the pole from the molecules, and by
arranging an apparatus so as to have the negative pole
movable and the body receiving the impact of the Radiant
Matter fixed, this recoil can be rendered sensible. In
appearance the apparatus (Fig. 12) is not unlike an ordinary

FIG. 12.

radiometer with aluminium disks for vanes, each disk coated
on one side with a film of mica. The fly is supported by
a hard steel instead of glass cup, and the needle point on
which it works is connected by means of a wire with a

platinum terminal sealed into the glass. At the top of the radiometer bulb a second terminal is sealed in. The radiometer therefore can be connected with an induction-coil, the movable fly being made the negative pole.

For these mechanical effects the exhaustion need not be so high as when phosphorescence is produced. The best pressure for this electrical radiometer is a little beyond that at which the dark space round the negative pole extends to the sides of the glass bulb. When the pressure is only a few millims. of mercury, on passing the induction current a halo of velvety violet light forms on the metallic side of the vanes, the mica side remaining dark. As the pressure diminishes, a dark space is seen to separate the violet halo from the metal. At a pressure of half a millim. this dark space extends to the glass, and rotation commences. On continuing the exhaustion the dark space further widens out and appears to flatten itself against the glass, when the rotation becomes very rapid.

Fig. 13.

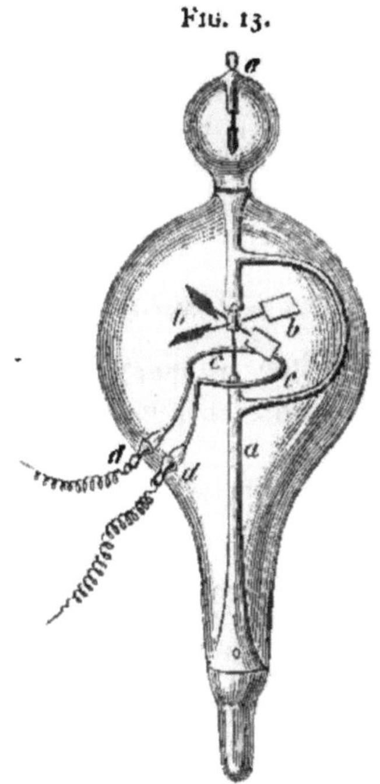

Here is another piece of apparatus (Fig. 13) which illustrates the mechanical force of the Radiant Matter from the negative pole. A stem (*a*) carries a needle-point in which revolves a light mica fly (*b b*). The fly consists of four square vanes of thin clear mica, supported on light aluminium arms, and in the centre is a small glass cap which rests on the needle-point. The vanes are inclined at an angle of 45° to the horizontal plane. Below the fly is a ring of fine platinum wire (*c c*), the ends of which pass through the glass at *d d*. An aluminium terminal (*e*) is sealed in at the top of the tube, and the whole is exhausted to a very high point.

By means of the electric lantern I project an image of the vanes on the screen. Wires from the induction-coil are attached, so that the platinum ring is made the negative pole, the aluminium wire (*e*) being positive. Instantly, owing to the projection of Radiant Matter from the platinum ring, the vanes rotate with extreme velocity. Thus far the apparatus has shown nothing more than the previous experiments have prepared us to expect; but observe what now happens. I disconnect the induction-coil altogether, and connect the two ends of the platinum wire with a small galvanic battery; this makes the ring *c c* red-hot, and under this influence you see that the vanes spin as fast as they did when the induction-coil was at work.

Here, then, is another most important fact. Radiant Matter in these high vacua is not only excited by the negative pole of an induction-coil, but a hot wire will set it in motion with force sufficient to drive round the sloping vanes.

Radiant Matter is deflected by a Magnet.

I now pass to another property of Radiant Matter. This long glass tube (Fig. 14), is very highly exhausted;

Fig. 14.

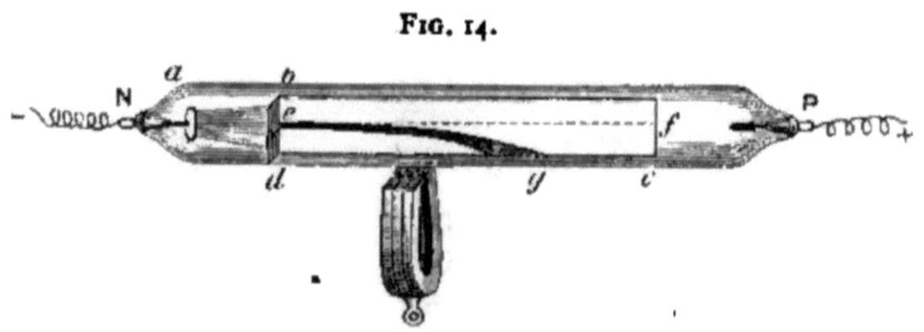

it has a negative pole at one end (*a*) and a long phosphorescent screen (*b*, *c*) down the centre of the tube. In front of the negative pole is a plate of mica (*b*, *d*) with a hole (*e*) in it, and the result is, when I turn on the current, a line of phosphorescent light (*e, f*) is projected along the whole length of the tube.   I now place beneath the tube a powerful horseshoe magnet: observe how the line of light (*e, g*) becomes curved under the magnetic influence waving about like a flexible wand as I move the magnet to and fro.

This action of the magnet is very curious, and if carefully followed up will elucidate other properties of Radiant Matter. Here (Fig. 15) is an exactly similar tube, but having at

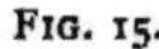

Fig. 15.

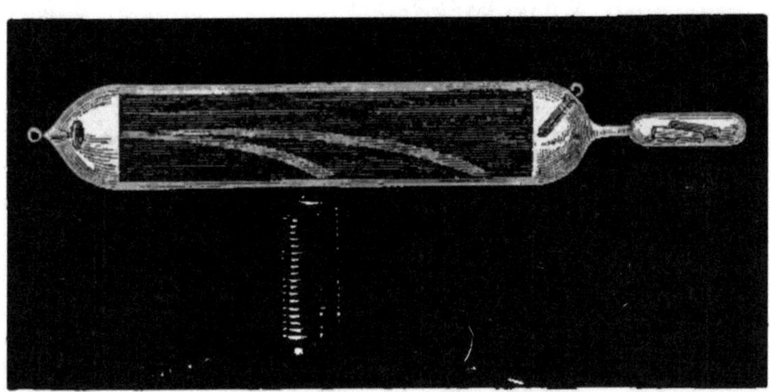

one end a small potash tube, which if heated will slightly injure the vacuum.   I turn on the induction current, and you see the ray of Radiant Matter tracing its trajectory in a curved line along the screen, under the influence of the horse-shoe magnet beneath.   Observe the shape of the curve.   The molecules shot from the negative pole may be likened to a discharge of iron bullets from a mitrailleuse, and the magnet beneath will represent the earth curving the trajectory of the shot by gravitation.   Here on this luminous screen you see the curved trajectory of the shot accurately traced.   Now suppose the deflecting force to remain constant, the curve traced by the projectile varies with the velocity.   If I put more powder in the gun the velocity will be greater and the trajectory flatter, and if I interpose a denser resisting medium between the gun and the target, I diminish the velocity of the shot, and thereby cause it to move in a greater curve and come to the ground sooner.   I cannot well increase before you the velocity of my stream of radiant molecules by putting more powder in my battery, but I will try and make them suffer greater resistance in their flight from one end of the tube to the other.   I heat the caustic potash with a spirit-lamp and so throw in a trace more gas. Instantly the stream of Radiant Matter responds. Its velocity is impeded, the magnetism has longer time on which to act on the individual molecules, the trajectory gets more and more curved, until, instead of shooting nearly to the end of the tube, my molecular bullets fall to the bottom before they have got more than half-way.

It is of great interest to ascertain whether the law governing the magnetic deflection of the trajectory of Radiant Matter is the same as has been found to hold good at a lower vacuum. The experiments I have just shown you were with a very high vacuum. Here is a tube with a low vacuum (Fig. 16). When I turn on

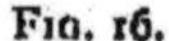

Fig. 16.

the induction spark, it passes as a narrow line of violet light joining the two poles. Underneath I have a powerful electro-magnet. I make contact with the magnet, and the line of light dips in the centre towards the magnet. I reverse the poles, and the line is driven up to the top of the tube. Notice the difference between the two phenomena. Here the action is temporary. The dip takes place under the magnetic influence; the line of discharge then rises and pursues its path to the positive pole. In the high exhaustion, however, after the stream of Radiant Matter had dipped to the magnet it did not recover itself, but continued its path in the altered direction.

By means of this little wheel, skilfully constructed by Mr. Gimingham, I am able to show the magnetic deflection in the electric lantern. The apparatus is shown in this diagram (Fig. 17). The negative pole (*a*, *b*) is in the form of a very shallow cup. In front of the cup is a mica screen (*c*, *d*), wide enough to intercept the Radiant Matter coming from the negative pole. Behind this screen is a mica wheel (*e*, *f*) with a series of vanes, making a sort of paddle-wheel. So arranged, the molecular rays from the pole *a b* will be cut off from the wheel, and will not produce any movement.

I now put a magnet, *g*, over the tube, so as to deflect the stream over or under the obstacle *c d*, and the result will be

Fig. 17.

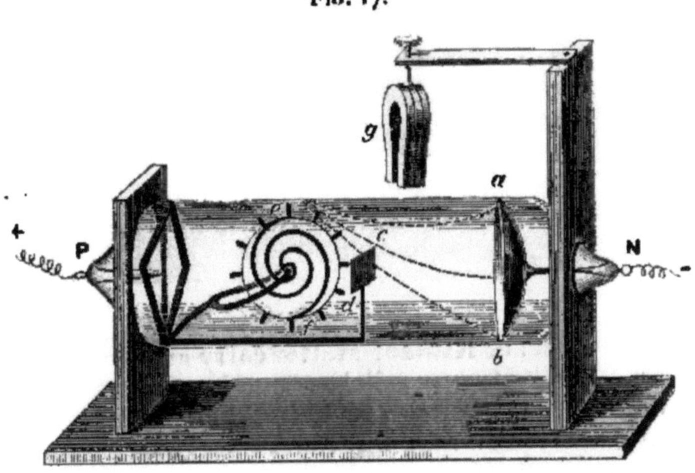

rapid motion in one or the other direction, according to the way the magnet is turned. I throw the image of the apparatus on the screen. The spiral lines painted on the wheel show which way it turns. I arrange the magnet to draw the molecular stream so as to beat against the upper vanes, and the wheel revolves rapidly as if it were an over-shot water-wheel. I turn the magnet so as to drive the Radiant Matter underneath; the wheel slackens speed, stops, and then begins to rotate the other way, like an under-shot water-wheel. This can be repeated as often as I reverse the position of the magnet.

I have mentioned that the molecules of the Radiant Matter discharged from the negative pole are negatively electrified. It is probable that their velocity is owing to the mutual repulsion between the similarly electrified pole and the molecules. In less high vacua, such as you saw a few minutes ago (Fig. 16), the discharge passes from one pole to another, carrying an electric current, as if it were a flexible wire. Now it is of great interest to ascertain if the stream of Radiant Matter from the negative pole also carries a current. Here (Fig. 18) is an apparatus which will decide the question at once. The tube contains two negative terminals (*a*, *b*) close together at one end, and one positive terminal (*c*) at the other. This enables me to send two streams of Radiant Matter side by side along the phosphorescent screen,—or by disconnecting one negative pole, only one stream.

Fig. 18.

If the streams of Radiant Matter carry an electric current they will act like two parallel conducting wires and attract one another; but if they are simply built up of negatively electrified molecules they will repel each other.

I will first connect the upper negative pole (*a*) with the coil, and you see the ray shooting along the line *d, f*. I now bring the lower negative pole (*b*) into play, and another line (*e, h*) darts along the screen. But notice the way the first line behaves; it jumps up from its first position, *d f*, to *d g*, showing that it is repelled, and if time permitted I could show you that the lower ray is also deflected from its normal direction: therefore the two parallel streams of Radiant Matter exert mutual repulsion, acting not like current carriers, but merely as similarly electrified bodies.

Radiant Matter produces heat when its motion is arrested.

During these experiments another property of Radiant Matter has made itself evident, although I have not yet drawn attention to it The glass gets very warm where the green phosphorescence is strongest. The molecular focus on the tube, which we saw earlier in the evening (Fig. 8) is intensely hot, and I have prepared an apparatus by which this heat at the focus can be rendered apparent to all present.

I have here a small tube (Fig. 19, *a*) with a cup-shaped negative pole. This cup projects the rays to a focus in the middle of the tube. At the side of the tube is a small electro-magnet, which I can set in action by touching a key, and the focus is then drawn to the

side of the glass tube (Fig. 19, *b*). To show the first
action of the heat I have coated the tube with wax.

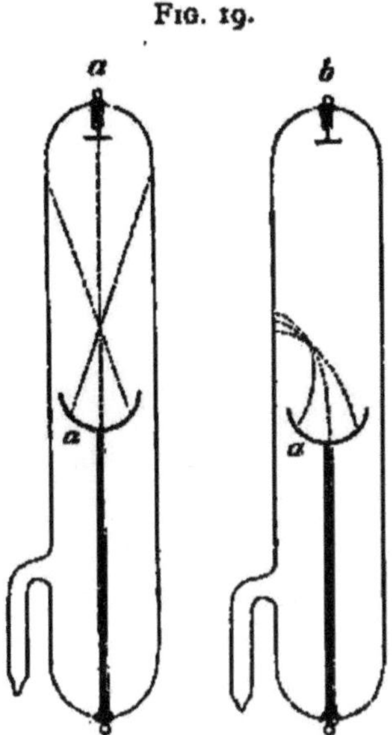

FIG. 19.

I will put the apparatus in front of the electric lantern
(Fig. 20, *d*), and throw a magnified image of the tube on
the screen. The coil is now at work, and the focus of
molecular rays is projected along the tube. I turn the
magnetism on, and draw the focus to the side of the glass.
The first thing you see is a small circular patch melted in
the coating of wax. The glass soon begins to disintegrate,
and cracks are shooting starwise from the centre of heat.
The glass is softening. Now the atmospheric pressure forces
it in, and now it melts. A hole (*e*) is perforated in the
middle, the air rushes in, and the experiment is at an end.

I can render this focal heat more evident if I allow
it to play on a piece of metal. This bulb (Fig. 21) is
furnished with a negative pole in the form of a cup (*a*).
The rays will therefore be projected to a focus on a piece
of iridio-platinum (*b*) supported in the centre of the bulb.

I first turn on the induction-coil slightly, so as not to bring
out its full power. The focus is now playing on the metal,
raising it to a white-heat. I bring a small magnet near,
and you see I can deflect the focus of heat just as I
did the luminous focus in the other tube. By shifting
the magnet I can drive the focus up and down, or draw it

Fig. 20.

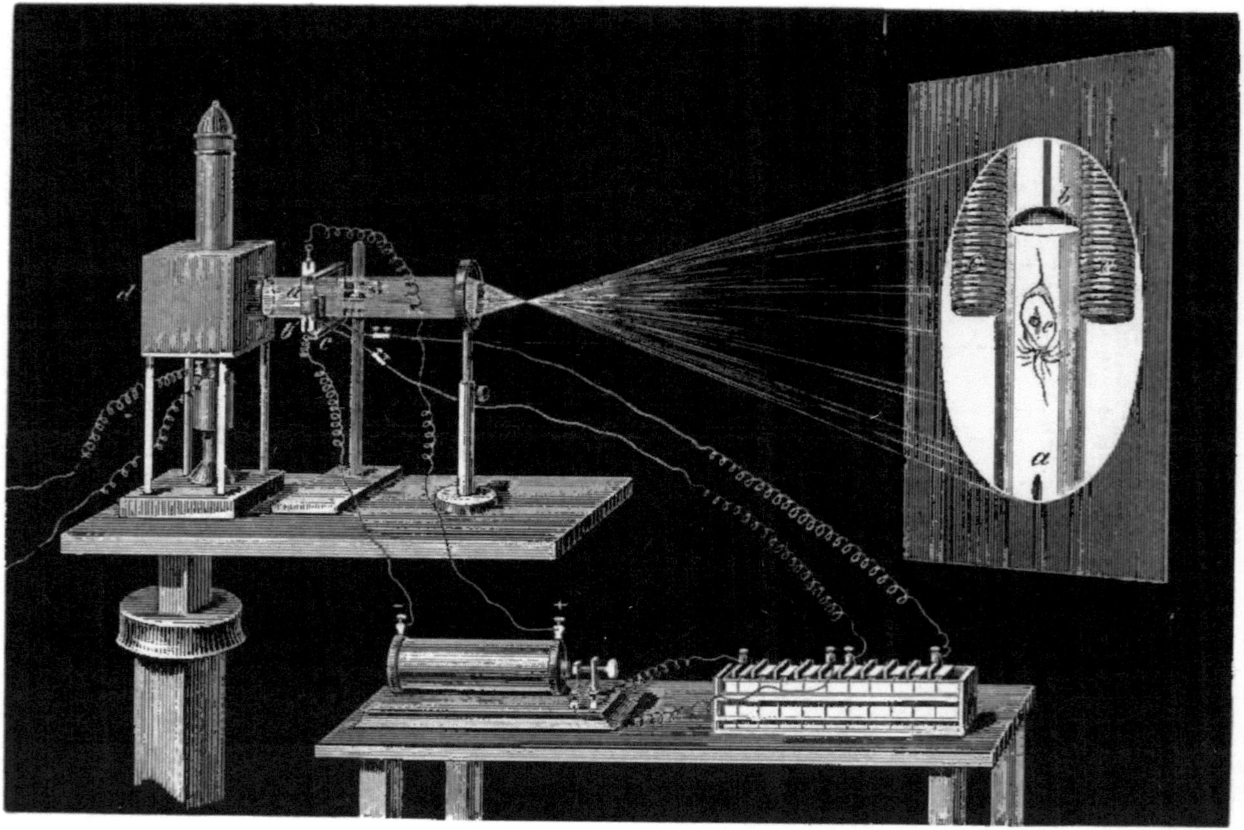

completely away from the metal, and leave it non-luminous.
I withdraw the magnet, and let the molecules have full

FIG 21.

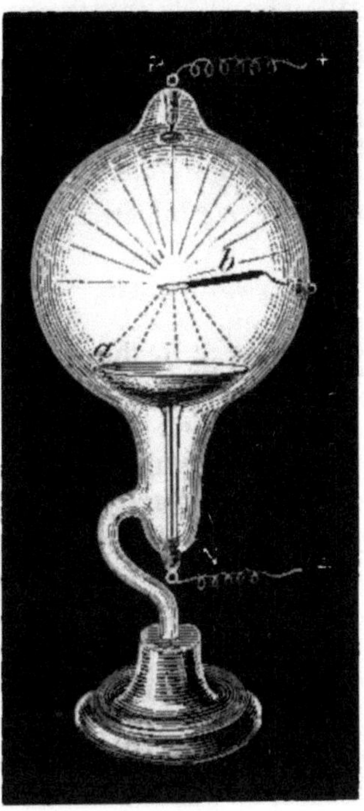

play again; the metal is now white-hot. I increase the
intensity of the spark. The iridio-platinum glows with almost insupportable brilliancy, and at last melts.

The Chemistry of Radiant Matter.

.   As might be expected, the chemical distinctions between
one kind of Radiant Matter and another at these high exhaustions are difficult to recognise. The physical properties I have been elucidating seem to be common to all
matter at this low density. Whether the gas originally
under experiment be hydrogen, carbonic acid, or atmospheric
air, the phenomena of phosphorescence, shadows, magnetic
deflection, &c., are identical, only they commence at
different pressures. Other facts however, show that at this
low density the molecules retain their chemical character-
istics. Thus by introducing into the tubes appropriate ab-
sorbents of residual gas, I can see that chemical attraction
goes on long after the attenuation has reached the best stage

for showing the phenomena now under illustration, and I am able by this means to carry the exhaustion to much higher degrees than I can get by mere pumping. Working with aqueous vapour I can use phosphoric anhydride as an absorbent; with carbonic acid, potash; with hydrogen, palladium; and with oxygen, carbon, and then potash. The highest vacuum I have yet succeeded in obtaining has been the 1-20,000,000th of an atmosphere, a degree which may be better understood if I say that it corresponds to about the hundredth of an inch in a barometric column three miles high.

It may be objected that it is hardly consistent to attach primary importance to the presence of *Matter*, when I have taken extraordinary pains to remove as much Matter as possible from these bulbs and these tubes, and have succeeded so far as to leave only about the one-millionth of an atmosphere in them. At its ordinary pressure the atmosphere is not very dense, and its recognition as a constituent of the world of Matter is quite a modern notion. It would seem that when divided by a million, so little Matter will necessarily be left that we may justifiably neglect the trifling residue and apply the term *vacuum* to space from which the air has been so nearly removed. To do so, however, would be a great error, attributable to our limited faculties being unable to grasp high numbers. It is generally taken for granted that when a number is divided by a million the quotient must necessarily be small, whereas it may happen that the original number is so large that its division by a million seems to make little impression on it. According to the best authorities, a bulb of the size of the one before you (13·5 centimetres in diameter) contains more than 1,000000,000000,000000,000000 (a quadrillion) molecules. Now, when exhausted to a millionth of an atmosphere we shall still have a trillion molecules left in the bulb—a number quite sufficient to justify me in speaking of the residue as *Matter*.

To suggest some idea of this vast number I take the exhausted bulb, and perforate it by a spark from the induction coil. The spark produces a hole of microscopical fineness, yet sufficient to allow molecules to penetrate and to destroy the vacuum. The inrush of air impinges against the vanes and sets them rotating after the manner of a windmill. Let us suppose the molecules to be of such a size that at every second of time a hundred millions could enter,

How long, think you, would it take for this small vessel to get full of air? An hour? A day? A year? A century? Nay, almost an eternity! A time so enormous that imagination itself cannot grasp the reality. Supposing this exhausted glass bulb, indued with indestructibility, had been pierced at the birth of the solar system; supposing it to have been present when the earth was without form and void; supposing it to have borne witness to all the stupendous changes evolved during the full cycles of geologic time, to have seen the first living creature appear, and the last man disappear; supposing it to survive until the fulfilment of the mathematicians' prediction that the Sun, the source of energy, four million centuries from its formation will ultimately become a burnt-out cinder;* supposing all this,—at the rate of filling I have just described, 100 million molecules a second—this little bulb even then would scarcely have admitted its full quadrillion of molecules.†

But what will you say if I tell you that all these molecules, this quadrillion of molecules, will enter through the microscopic hole before you leave this room? The hole being unaltered in size, the number of molecules undiminished, this apparent paradox can only be explained by again supposing the size of the molecules to be diminished almost infinitely—so that instead of entering at the rate of 100 millions every second, they troop in at a rate of something like 300 trillions a second. I have done the sum, but figures when they mount so high cease to have any meaning, and such calculations are as futile as trying to count the drops in the ocean.

In studying this Fourth state of Matter we seem at length to have within our grasp and obedient to our control

---

* The possible duration of the Sun from formation to extinction has been variously estimated by different authorities, at from 18 million years to 400 million years. For the purpose of this illustration I have taken the highest estimate.

† According to Mr. Johnstone Stoney (Phil. Mag., vol. 36. p. 141), 1 c.c. of air contains about 1000,000000,000000,000000 molecules. Therefore a bulb 13·5 centims. diameter contains $13 \cdot 5^3 \times 0 \cdot 5236 \times 1000,000000,000000,000000$ or 1,288252.350000,000000,000000 molecules of air at the ordinary pressure. Therefore the bulb when exhausted to the millionth of an atmosphere contains 1,288252,350000,000000 molecules, leaving 1,288251,061747,650000,000000 molecules to enter through the perforation. At the rate of 100,000000 molecules a second, the time required for them all to enter will be

12882,510617,476500 seconds, or

214,708510,291275 minutes, or

3·578475,171521 hours, or

149103,132147 days, or

408 501731 years.

the little indivisible particles which with good warrant are
supposed to constitute the physical basis of the universe.
We have seen that in some of its properties Radiant Matter
is as material as this table, whilst in other properties it
almost assumes the character of Radiant Energy.   We
have actually touched the border land where Matter and
Force seem to merge into one another, the shadowy realm
between Known and Unknown which for me has always had
peculiar temptations.   I venture to think that the greatest
scientific problems of the future will find their solution in
this Border Land, and even beyond; here, it seems to me,
lie Ultimate Realities, subtle, far-reaching, wonderful.

> " Yet all these were, when no Man did them know,
>   Yet have from wisest Ages hidden beene ;
> And later Times thinges more unknowne shall show.
>   Why then should witlesse Man so much misweene,
>   That nothing is, but that which he hath seene ?"

London : Printed by E. J. Davey, Boy Court, Ludgate Hill, E.C.